THE BOY,

AND

THE WITCHES OF SALEM

BY

SHEILA WHYMAN

Chapter One

The Freak!

"Freak!" the rabble of childish faces shouted.

"Freak! Freak! FREAK!" they chanted, in an ever increasing crescendo. Sharp fingers jabbed at him, hard kicks bruised his scrawny legs, hands pushed, shoulders jostled, taunts hurt. James hid his face, covered his head, and crouched, hiding his body, as if the ground might mercifully; swallow him up into a giant, dark chasm. The adults passively looked on in horror whilst the jeering children laughed and taunted more; Cruel words, cruel names, cruel world.....

This was James Tyler's world; Malicious and unkind, alone and unloved. Was he a freak? Well of course he was. Had he not been told this every day, for the past ten years? Was he not reminded regularly by children and adults alike and worst of all by his parents? Yet inside James was an ordinary boy, with ordinary feelings and ordinary needs and longings. He could not help the pitiless fate that had made him different. He could not help his extraordinary appearance. All he had to do was live with it, accept it, stand proud and believe in himself. But inside the outer shell, lay only loneliness and fear, not bravery and strength. Cruel fate, cruel form, cruel world...

James, who had endured enough, pushed aside the crowd and ran helter-skelter, as fast as his small legs would carry him, home to the house in the open fields off Ipswich Road: His snow white hair trailed in the wind behind him, like the mane of a ghostly unicorn. His startling, pink eyes darted from left to right, tracing his homeward journey: His pale, translucent body sped past fading houses and trees. Sanctuary beckoned. There would be no solace in his mother's words, of course, only unkind jibes. His father would ignore him, as he always did. His elder sister would look on with a pained expression in her eyes. James would seek out his bolt hole in the barn and therein would find peace and calm. There, inside the cocoon he had made for himself, would lie a brief respite.

Reaching the barn, James thankfully avoided the accusing, ignoring, pained eyes of his family. He settled in the hay, dry-eyed, staring at the rafters, not able to cry because his pain went beyond tears. He had learned long ago that crying only brought more pain, more suffering, more accusations. He felt dry inside, his heart curled into a tight ball, like a frightened hedgehog.

No-one would reach in through those prickles. No-one loved James and James loved no-one in return. Saddened, he lay quiet and still, whilst the unkind jeers rang in his ears – Freak! Freak! Freak! He shut them out, ignoring the wrenching pain. Then, as he closed his eyes, he forced himself to sleep, the cruel, pitiless world left behind while he dreamed silently of a bright, accepting one. If only dreams came true. If only everyone accepted him for what he was. If only he could change his appearance, but life could not be lived on if only. It had to be endured. Cruel world, cruel people, cruel, cruel fate.

Chapter Two

Accusation and Punishment

Waking, James heard his mother's voice long before she appeared inside the barn, the shrill edge to her words was familiar.

"James Tyler, I want to see you, right now!" she demanded.

He knew he was in trouble. What terrible crime had he committed now? Was being alive not crime enough? If he just lay here, ignored her, pretended he could not hear her, would she go away? He was sure she would not. James grimaced and braced himself for the coming tirade of blame which his mother undoubtedly had in store for him. He eased himself down from his hiding place and faced his mother's stiffly held body.

Mrs Tyler was an upright, god-fearing woman, her simple but functional dress and neatly coiled hair paid homage to her Puritan upbringing, hard work and duty to God, her sole reason for living: she stood stark and tall, like a great, winter oak.

Now, her face was twisted into an accusing scowl that was aimed directly at James.

"Reverend Parris says you have been provoking the village children   again," Mrs Tyler bit out in a furious whisper.

James knew better than to contradict his mother so stood head down, repenting a crime he did not commit. His small body sagged. what punishment was his to endure this time?

"Children should be seen but not heard, James Tyler. You have encouraged others to shout out and make a public display of themselves," she continued. "For this you will do without supper this evening and go straight way to your bed and pray to God for forgiveness."

James knew too well what was expected from the children of the village but it was never their fault that they jeered and shouted at him in the street. The blame always belonged to him, the freak, the boy who had no colour, no friends, no place in this world. However, for this relatively light punishment, James was truly thankful.

Mrs Tyler pulled herself up to what seemed an enormous height, outstretched her arm and pointed in the direction of the house.

"To bed, James Tyler. And God forgive you for your wicked ways," she said in a controlled, contorted voice.

James moved off, head down, silent. He never tried to defend himself, argue against the injustice of the accusations, what was the use? No-one believed in him, no-one was on his side. It did not matter what he said, he was always in the wrong, he was always the perpetrator of these evil crimes. He was a freak after all: A living punishment for his parents' past wickedness, they constantly reminded him, Satan's work! The only way they could earn forgiveness was to make sure that he learned to be dutiful and god-fearing, just like his mother. Soon James reached his room and entered. Night was falling. He was not allowed a candle and as darkness came, it closed around him like a security blanket. When the light was gone and no-one could see him, James felt protected when his differences were hidden. With this thought and ignoring the rumbles of his empty stomach, James undressed, got into bed and awaited another day, perhaps a better one might arrive tomorrow. The world always looked better tomorrow! As these thoughts drifted through his mind, he heard the distinctive sound of the lock on his door, being turned.

Chapter Three

A Change in the Air

And so the new day came. His face in the window bore witness to the fact that nothing had changed. That was the problem, nothing ever changed, tomorrow never really came, it was always today. James dressed and ventured quietly to his door. He listened to the silence. Perhaps no-one would bother with him today. Turning, he had moved no more than a few footsteps away from the door when a hand touched his shoulder. He spun around, fright gripping his body, and looked straight into the solemn eyes of his sister, Rebecca. She pressed her finger against her lips and gestured through the open door, towards two figures huddled together at the kitchen table. Their mother and father were deep in hushed conversation, more whispers, more accusations, more lies. Rebecca smiled. She handed him two chunks of fresh bread, pointed towards the outside door and disappeared as silently as she had arrived.

James knew that he must also disappear before his parents became aware of his waking. Rebecca was not a friend, but neither was she the enemy. Whether she loved James was still uncertain, but she certainly did not despise him, like so many others. Rebecca's advice was born out of pity and James knew better than to ignore it. So he crept with soft steps towards the outer door, not daring to breathe. If he did, then surely a great ice storm would be let loose and his mother would again curse him in that oh so quiet, controlled voice, his father looking on, his body as frozen as the words from his wife's mouth. Escape beckoned.

James carefully eased his body through the half-open outer door and immediately felt warmed by the rays of the August sun. His white hair glowed gold and his pale skin warmed with a pink sheen, his eyes darkened and could almost be called amber. The fields danced in front of his eyes. The day was glorious. James half smiled. Today WOULD be a better day. He would lie in the fields, hidden. He would not play; even he knew that was forbidden. He imagined himself wandering the open spaces, alone, no-one to chastise him, criticize or ridicule him, just him, alone in the fields.

This thought of freedom firmly fixed, James walked, no almost skipped to the fields he could see. When he was a safe distance from the house, he threw himself down amongst the crops, rolled to face the sun and smiled, happy for now. Today was his. And although he would not venture into the village, he would not go back to the house either. He would stay here in the fields forever. Rye laughter escaped from his mouth then was quickly swallowed for fear of being heard. Joy was so strange. Why it had happened today, James did not know. Maybe it was the thought of new tomorrows. Maybe it was Rebecca's unexpected kindness. Maybe it was just the escape for a day when no-one would know where to look for him. Whatever the reason, joy filled James, bubbling to the surface like the air from golden fish gills.

Cheered by his imagination, James set off, on his lonely adventure. As he walked, he chewed the bread and smiled again at his sister's defiance. He hoped she would not be punished too harshly for her small kindness. James knew that trouble was likely, when their parents discovered her crime. Pushing this thought to the back of his mind, he smiled in the knowledge that today was destined to be special. It felt different,, he felt different, not in a bad way, not like his appearance. James felt the draw of something magical, a change in the air.

Chapter Four

The Hidden Box

James wandered aimlessly for half a day and it felt good. Now he found himself in the small, familiar wood, near to the village. The air smelt of flowers and grass and comfort. He decided to rest against the trunk of a large tree. He sank to the floor, feeling the bulk of the bark against his back. Well, what to do now? He wanted the day to last forever.

For no reason, he started to draw circles around and around on the ground beside him, his brain mesmerized by the soothing movement as more and more of the earth was pushed to the side by his circling hand. Time stopped. The movement transfixed him and his eyes began to droop whilst his hand continued, almost of its own accord, burrowing deeper into the soft ground. James felt himself drifting into a half sleep, the feeling of the warm earth on his hand, drawing him into a dream. Something called to him, someone whispered his name then all was quiet.

James woke with a start. How long had he slept, weary from his wanderings? When he looked up, the sun still flickered through the leaves of the trees. When he looked around, it seemed only minutes since he had arrived. But when he looked down, he was not quite prepared for what he saw. For there, next to him was a huge, gaping hole, earth pushed to the sides in untidy heaps and at the bottom of the hole, lay a wooden box. It looked like a treasure box. James just stared. Had something led him to this box? It seemed strange that he should find it so easily.   Was this an accident or fate? He did not know, but he felt compelled by some force to investigate it.

The box moved when James tugged at it with both hands. Then gently lifting it from the hole, he placed it on the grass in front of him. The urge to open the box was enormous, but James was not sure. He had heard dark tales of magic and witchcraft in this wood. He had been included in some of those stories, as if he was the instigator of the magic. Was he just fulfilling his destiny by opening this strange box?

"Don't be ridiculous, James Tyler," he whispered, for a moment sounding exactly like his mother. "You are no more a witch than is your mother." This idea was even more ridiculous than thoughts of magic! So James carefully dusted the grains of dirt off the top of the box and opened it.

He had expected to find at least a few gold coins or jewelry in there. He had thought perhaps robbers had buried their ill-gotten gains here.   This seemed the most obvious explanation.   However, there were no such things inside. Instead, there were just books and papers.   On the top lay a red book with a bright gold pattern on its front cover: Underneath a variety of other books and carefully rolled papers. James decided to investigate further, to read the red book, if he was able.   He was not a good reader.   Well, there really was no reason that he should be. His mother could not read and his father recognized a few words.   They learned their bible passages from the reverend at church.   Rebecca had not been taught to read either.   There was no good reason for girls to learn. However, Mr Tyler, an aspiring businessman, planned to be one of those rich merchants in the town, so he had reluctantly paid for James to be taught.   Despite James' appearance and in order to win acceptance, Mr Tyler had no other choice than to be seen to be educating his only son. So, James had begun to learn the basics. He hoped that this would be enough to make sense of what was contained in the red book.

Shaking, James lifted the book from the box. Desperate: He wanted to open it, but he was scared. What if this was a bad thing. His mother would surely say it was. He could almost hear her:

"James Tyler, you wicked boy. You are the devil's own work. The book does not belong to you. It is not yours to open. Put it back, at once!"

Then another voice crept into his mind.

"Open it," it breathed. "Open it now!" The one voice became a chorus, tempting, tantalizing, begging!

The book began to slowly slip from James' agitated fingers and too late, fell open, forcing James to see into it.

At that moment James, expected a bolt to wing its way from heaven and shatter his body into a million pieces.

"Wicked boy!" He heard his mother's uncharacteristic scream. Would the devil appear? Would God strike him dead? James closed his eyes, waiting. Nothing happened.

Forcing one eye open, James stared at the page in front of him. The other eye followed suit and when James focussed on the black print, he gasped. "No!" The sound escaped and echoed around the silent wood. James Tyler was dumbfounded. He looked at the writing on the page again. His meagre grasp of the written word was not at fault. The word he had immediately recognized WAS 'spell'.

Chapter Five

Shock and Near Discovery

Poring over the book, James struggled to decipher all of the words, but he understood enough to make some sense of what was written there. The word spell was not the greatest shock in store for him, however: For as he read on, it became clear that what he had found was actually a book full of spells. Not one recipe for wickedness, but many. James was both intrigued and terrified. What should he do? Was he already damned for having opened the book? Could he stop now? Did he want to stop? Questions chased through his mind: Questions with no answers: Questions he dared not answer!

How long James sat staring at the book was not certain, but gradually the light through the trees changed to a half light and then to total darkness. Still James stared at the book, questions repeated without answers. Finally, dazed and without clear thought, he quickly placed the book in the box, closed the lid firmly and threw the box back into the hole. His fingers worked relentlessly, without pause, as they scraped dirt from the untidy piles back into the hole. Faster and faster his hands moved to conceal what he had found. When the hole was filled, he stood, looked over his shoulder then scraped over the newly disturbed earth with his foot, trying to hide the terrible discovery.

James ran home as fast as his legs would run, as if the devil himself were chasing him. In his mind's eye, he imagined a great black stallion with wild eyes, pursuing him, trampling the ground, racing to trample him too. Scared? James was terrified. His mother's ever accusing words rang in his ears: "James Tyler, you wicked, wicked boy. You are the devil's own work!" The voice grated on and on: "Wicked... devil's work... wicked boy... James Tyler...wicked, wicked, wicked!" The words pounded in a punishing rhythm, in time with his feet, with his heartbeat, with the thundering hooves of the imagined black stallion.

On reaching his home, James sped straight for his hiding place in the barn. But his bolt hole was denied him this time. For there standing tall and straight, her rigid body silhouetted in the doorway, was his mother. In her hand a sharp light gleamed from an oil lamp, her face ghostly and menacing in that light. Her eyes bored into James' ashen face. Could she see the reflection of the red book in his eyes? Did she know?

"James Tyler, you wicked boy." She began, echoing the words that had chased him from the wood. "What is this wickedness you have been up to today?" She knew. She knew.

James closed his eyes. He shivered and clenched his fists.

"I know... that you bewitched your sister into helping you this morning. I know that you have not carried out your chores today. I know that you have returned and tried to slip away without saying your prayers." She paused, as if the terrible weight of his sins might shatter her.

"James Tyler, you will go straight to your bed. You will say prayers for one hour. And you will stay in your room until you are asked to leave. Is that clear?" Mrs Tyler could hardly contain her anger, her temper rose as her face contorted in the light shining from the lamp.

"And..... James Tyler... Be thankful that your father is not here to take a stick and beat you for your sins!"

James was thankful. He was very thankful, because it was quite clear, that his mother did not know the half of his wickedness today.

Chapter Six

The Return to the Wood

James knew before the sun's rays had begun to stream through his window that he would go back to the wood. He had laid awake for most of the night, reliving his discovery, and his fear: Justifying his actions. He had concluded that as everyone believed he was already lost, then he could not become more wicked by reading the book and using the spells. Making this last choice had taken some courage, even to think about it was frightening, but he knew that using the spells was his destiny. How he knew, he was not sure. Something called to him from that box. Something still urged him to go on. Something told him it was meant to be.

Today there was no Rebecca to rescue him from his room. Not long after sunrise, hearing a faint click at his door and fearing his mother's anger, he dutifully knelt at his bedside and gave up a prayer. It was a prayer of hope and defiance. It asked for forgiveness and permission. It affirmed his belief in the magic found in the wood and that it was his destiny to use it. Opening the door and finding her son deep in prayer convinced Mrs Tyler that he was truly repentant. Standing at the entrance to his bedroom, her face glowed with smug satisfaction. It was so easy to bring her son back into line. She smiled. James was so easy to chastise and then dismiss from her mind. She would deliver threats of great punishment for his sins and in return he would always obey. She liked that! Then she would forget he existed and continue on in her dutiful way. She felt no tinge of regret or remorse. This had to be done, if James was to be saved. This had to be done, if SHE was to be saved.

She continued to smile. Perhaps she would allow him to hide himself away once his chores were done. Perhaps she would then forget him and sit with Rebecca, talking and sewing and making plans. This seemed such a good idea that she turned to James and smiled, He immediately reeled back in shock. His mother never really looked at him, just at the distance beyond his right shoulder. What was she thinking? James thought he did not really want to know.

"James Tyler, your chores await you," his mother's voice brought him back with a jolt. "And after your chores, you may have a small rest until your meal is ready." What was she thinking? His mother had never allowed such a thing, However, he was not about to argue, so he scuttled off to carry out his chores, as quickly as he could, thoughts of the wood and the box and the magic not far from his mind.

The small rest became an adventure. Chores done, he sneaked off to the wood to rediscover the box. He found the tree and the newly dug dirt easily. His hands clawed and scraped and pushed the earth aside... and there it was...the treasure box. Quickly he opened it and removed the red book. He was just about to close the lid and return the box to the ground, when a silver glint caught his eye. He peered deep into the box. A chain lay hidden under the papers. He pulled at it... and to his surprise a cat shaped pendant appeared at the end of the chain, reflecting the sun's rays onto his face. He turned it in his hand. On the back of the cat shape, someone had roughly engraved the initials J.T. What a strange object. What a strange inscription. He stuffed the pendant into his pocket and hid the red book in the sack he had brought with him. He knelt quickly and concealed the box once more in its hiding place. Intending to read the spell book in the barn, James set off with a spring to his step and lightness in his heart. Halfway home, he suddenly stopped, a peculiar thought entering his head, halting his feet.

"Those are my initials!" he whispered into the breeze. "The pendant must belong to me." And with that he smiled a real smile for the first time in his entire life.

Chapter Seven

A Dream Come True

Back in the barn, James carefully removed the red book from the sack. He had just opened it, when he heard the voice he dreaded. His mother's sharp tone reached his unwelcoming ears, but the words were not yet quite clear. He did not really need to hear the words. He knew his mother was calling him to his midday meal. After all, she only promised a short rest and his visit to the woods and the recovery of the book seemed to have taken ages. Too long! Reluctantly, he replaced the book and eased himself down. Better that his mother did not find him here. She might have wanted to know what he was up to. He was not sure that he could have hidden the truth from her a second time.

So, James moved slowly back to the house, heavy footed, knowing that the magic would have to wait. The midday meal progressed as usual. Father said prayers, giving endless thanks for their food and their good fortune: And looking directly at James, asked forgiveness for their sins. Then Rebecca and his mother served the bread and cheese, whilst his father sat silent. Thus, he continued for the remainder of the mealtime.

There was no friendly conversation at this table. Eating over, James' father stood, bade a stern farewell to his wife and daughter, ignored James and went about his business for the afternoon. James had no idea what that entailed.

Rebecca and his mother began clearing away and washing the dishes. If James was lucky he might be able to borrow some more time this afternoon to continue his adventure. A thought occurred to him. Would his mother allow it? Would she listen? He rarely spoke directly to either of his parents, never really starting a conversation. They preferred it that way. So James would need to sound natural, as if he always talked freely. His heart beat faster. He practised a smile; No that definitely would not do. Well, here goes anyway. The worst she could say was no. He dared not think of the worst she could do, for fear of losing his nerve.

"Mother." Hardly a sound passed James' lips. He cleared his throat. This time the sound was so loud that he thought that they would both turn and stare. But no, they carried on with their chores, as if nothing had happened.

"Mother." James said as firmly as he could. This time she turned abruptly and fixed James with a straight eye, which then moved to a distance beyond his shoulder. He knew that she was already beginning to dismiss him, so he spoke loudly and quickly before she could ignore him again.

"Mother. I would like to go and practise my reading. My tutor says that I must practise if I am to make my father proud of me." Not strictly the truth, but neither was it a lie. His tutor had told him to practise, but he surely meant reading the bible, not a spell book!

His mother fixed him to the spot with a stare. Was she trying to see if he was telling the truth? Then, turning away, she answered,

"James Tyler, you may. But be sure to be back before sunset to carry out your chores." James could not quite believe his luck. He knew today was different, but this was too much. However, he was not going to waste such an opportunity, so careful not to draw further attention to himself, he walked slowly to the outer door and then to the barn.

The sack and book were just as he had left them and the pendant still lay inside his pocket. He removed the book from its hiding place and opened it. He still could not quite believe that this book spoke of magic. Perhaps it was a trick. Someone was probably laughing at him right now. Maybe even the girls in the village. He did not care! He was going to choose a spell and try it. What had he got to lose? Nothing could make his life worse than it already was.

Turning to a well-thumbed page, James began to read. It took a while for him to understand. Some of the words were beyond his basic knowledge. Eventually, though, he worked out that he needed to wear the cat pendant and say some words. Then, and this was the exciting part, especially for him, the spell would change his appearance. Oh, how he longed for that. This was his dream. This was his destiny.

Chapter Eight

The Transformation

Before he could change his mind or his mother could call him back to the house, James quickly put on the shiny pendant. It was heavy around his neck. Was this a test? Was this too heavy for him to bear? Shaking free of these dark thoughts, he again looked at the words in the book. Doubt filled his mind. The words were unfamiliar and awkward on his lips. What if he got them wrong? The spell may then spin him away into the unknown. Harsh as his life seemed, it was far better than being alone and stranded somewhere he did not know. Where the expectations of others were uncertain. At least here, he knew the score...

James faltered: Looked again at the words: Looked upwards in hope of some sign that he should go on. At that moment, he heard the crunching footsteps of his father as he passed the barn, on the way back to the house. This might be his only chance. Soon he would be called in to carry out his chores. Then he may never be given another opportunity. The footsteps were a sign. He must go on. He grasped the pendant in his hand and whispered unsteadily, the words printed in the book...

"Magic….. Invades….. All…. Our….. Worlds….!"
They were meaningless to him, but he said them all the same. What if they were wrong? He had no way of knowing. Panic gripped. What if they were wrong! James shut his eyes and prayed. This time he prayed for mercy!

The sound of the deep voice, which belonged to his father, shocked him back to reality. The voice seemed to be talking directly to him. His father never spoke to him: Never even acknowledged his existence. The voice was gentle, warming; cajoling sounds rather than actual words. He slowly opened his eyes and in disbelief saw his father's face peering down at him. The unexpected sensation of being raised in the air, then inspected in great detail was unnerving. The dark eyes scanned his face and that familiar hard mouth suddenly broadened into a huge smile. It was surely not for him! James felt uncomfortable, weak. This was a genuine smile, not the hard grimace he usually saw on his father's face. Listening more carefully, he began to hear words he recognized.

"What a beautiful example of God's creation you are," the voice cooed. "Such a blessing to be bestowed upon us today. Are you also a good mouser, I wonder? Will you sleep here in my barn and earn your keep, if I let you stay?" James heard the words, but the meaning escaped him. Had his father gone completely mad?

James saw one of the big, work-roughened hands which belonged to his father descend slowly towards him. Oh No! James was terrified. What had he done now to deserve a beating? But the hand softened into a gentle stroke along his back and James was stilled into silent shock. His father was surely mad. Crazed by the wickedness of his son? James stared at the smiling figure. Perhaps he had fallen asleep and was dreaming. Perhaps, in desperation, his mind had conjured up a kind and loving father. Then a thought struck, sudden and mind numbing. Perhaps the spell had worked!

Incredibly, he realized, the spell HAD worked and his appearance had changed. Could this be true? His father's words returned in his memory... beautiful... creature... a blessing! His father had used these words to describe HIM! The spell had worked. Joy spread through his bones. His appearance had changed. He was no longer the freak! He was beautiful, blessed...accepted. Then another memory returned... 'a mouser. Mouser?' What did that mean? James knew of only one creature known as a mouser and that was... A CAT?. As James discovered, the spell had worked. He had turned into a beautiful, snow-white cat, with the amber eyes and silky coat of a celebrated winner. He smiled. He was living his dream!

Chapter Nine

Snowflake – Cat or Boy

The snow-white cat lived a charmed life in the Tyler household. All who met him loved him. paid him attention and never, but never referred to him as a freak. James spent more and more time as the cat, they named Snowflake. Even his father smiled at the fanciful name. Unfortunately the smile was beyond his mother, who tolerated the animal because she believed it worked hard keeping the harvest mice at bay. Nevertheless, she saved the tastiest morsels of food and the creamiest cream for the creature. James savoured every moment, every morsel, every last drop of cream!

Rebecca fell in love with Snowflake the moment she saw him and James, disguised as the cat had followed wherever she led. Summer turned to autumn and James found peace in the life of 'the mouser'! Once chores were done, the spell was spoken and Snowflake spent happy and blissful hours in the company of his family. Whether they missed James was uncertain, but no-one ever mentioned that he only appeared at chore and meal times. Whether they noticed the complaints from the village had lessened, they did not say. Life went on and James was almost content.

However, the memories of the taunts and cruel words never quite faded from his mind. He still railed against the cruel fate that made him live another, secret life. Nighttime now, became his enemy. Whereas before, the night hid his difference, now the difference manifested itself in his dreams. The taunts, the jibes, the cruel words echoed through nightmares, as if a message was being sent to him. He woke each morning, hot and feverish, escaping the dark images of children and adults, who would never let him forget. The spell had won him acceptance, but it did not mean that he would be welcomed as himself. Whenever the human James appeared he was greeted with the same sneers and accusations of wickedness. What would they say if they knew his secret? Then he would surely be labelled the
devil's work!

So the dream was not as perfect as he imagined. Undoubtedly his life was better than before. He did not regret the day he had found the spell book. He just wished that he could change forever. If only, one day, he awoke to find that he was no longer James Tyler, then that would be magic. These thoughts worried James. Was he giving into wickedness by wanting more? More than he had already been given. He had never thought of himself as selfish, but those who constantly wanted were surely not only selfish but wicked. His mother would certainly agree with that.

With these concerns in mind, James decided that although he would still use the spell, he would also try again, to win acceptance as himself. This time he would try harder. His newfound confidence, he knew, came from the life he spent as Snowflake: But whether he was cat or boy, he was still James Tyler, wasn't he? He was still the same person inside. Surely if he worked hard enough, others would see through his unusual appearance to the boy within. James was filled with new hope and willingness to try. He would convince everyone that he was a worthy part of their life and the village. He was NOT a freak, but an individual with feelings and hopes and dreams. The decision was made. Action would be taken! After that, James took up a life, half cat, half boy.

Chapter Ten

The Final Torment!

James was soon to find that what you dreamt in your heart was not as easy to make real. He tried. Oh, how he had tried! Each day, he awoke. Each day his confidence whittled to nothing, like the wood of an inexperienced carver. He was tempted. He was sorely tempted to spend all of his life as the cat! What would it matter? Who would care? It was certain that no-one would miss James Tyler, the boy: The freak! The taunts began again, but this time they seemed more cruel, more unendurable. The children in the village took every opportunity to measure out his differences, his inadequacies: To march them up and down in front of friend and stranger alike. Today was the worst!

James had been sent to the village to collect flour, so that his mother could bake more bread. He had not wanted to go. He knew what awaited him. Abigail Williams and her group of friends waited. These girls were particularly cruel, today was no exception. As he walked down the main street towards the mill, he could see the gang of girls outside, talking. It was not long before they spotted him. They had not waited for him to draw near but had begun their jibes as he approached.

"Here comes the freak!" shouted Abigail, as her friends laughed and nudged one another. Elizabeth Parris, the reverend's daughter sneered, her lips drawn back over her teeth. She was the cruellest of them all! Her jibes hit home.

"Where did your parents find you, freak, in their garden with the other slugs and worms?" Her words hurt, afresh, even though they had been said a thousand times before. "Did they take pity and give you a home?" Her face contorted into mock pity. She turned to her friends and whispered in an exaggerated, quiet tone, "I hear his mother hates him, can't bear to look at his face." The others sniggered and stared fixedly at him. "And his father.... Well I heard him say that they would sell him to the highest bidder! Imagine that!".
The taunts and comments continued, as James grew nearer. No-one came to his defence. No-one denied the words that Elizabeth was saying. No-one stopped to notice! Elizabeth and Abigail continued. Looking directly at James, Abigail said, "Want to know a secret, Betty?" Elizabeth Parris stared at James.

"Is it about the freak?" she replied, never taking her eyes from James.

"Course it is," Abigail smiled. "She lowered her voice to a conspiratorial   tone. "James, the freak, Tyler has a dark secret." She pointed a finger at James, then drawing it back she placed it across her smiling lips.

James stood transfixed. Did she know? Had she seen him? The horror of the taunts gave way to the horror of Abigail's revelation. All the girls now stared at James, awaiting the 'dark secret'. James could not move. Abigail did not immediately speak. She waited, drawing out the effect of her words: Drawing out James' agony. Then, in a great rush of words she revealed....

"James Tyler has a girlfriend!" She laughed aloud, as if this was cause for huge merriment.

"JAMES TYLER... has a girlfriend!" she stretched the last word out in shocked disbelief. "He meets her in the woods. I've heard them talking. I've heard him whisper 'sweet talk' to her! In the woods!" Abigail snorted.

"A girlfriend?" the others mocked.

"Surely no-one wants a freak?" Elizabeth sneered. "You must be joking!" At that, they all laughed and began to whisper more quietly, so that James could not hear.

James was furious. How dare they? How dare they mock him! How dare they scare him like that? Anger bubbled up inside him, a swift anger never felt before. He supposed the shock of finding that the secret was so stupid compared to his real secret had brought about this reaction. He never felt anger, only hurt! His blood pressure rose, his vision turned red, his fingers clenched into fists. This time he would not walk away. This time they had gone too far. He, to his surprise, wanted revenge. No-more hurting in secret! No more lying dry-eyed in the barn. He knew exactly what he was going to do. He was going to scare THEM!

Chapter Eleven

The Revenge Begins

James knew exactly what he wanted to do. Even when he had returned home with the flour, he still knew exactly what he wanted to do. He had calmed considerably by then, but revenge had never left his mind. James was determined. Those girls would pay dearly for their cruelty. He would scare them. He would scare them until they begged for mercy. In his mind's eye, he could already see the horror on their faces. He could already hear their sobs. He could feel their pain! Had he not been that way himself? He smiled. Was he also cruel? No, THEY, unlike him, deserved their punishment.

Next time James ventured into the village, it was not as himself. He had waited until the following day for the opportunity to begin his payback. Minutes ago, in the barn, he had quickly turned from boy to cat and emerged into the sunlight as Snowflake, white and pure. Up until now, he had never gone farther than the house and garden in his transformed state, not even into the fields unless accompanied by his sister. Now he boldly trotted towards the village, revenge still uppermost in his mind. Of course, the villagers were as taken with the cat, as his family were. He knew this would be so. Wherever he went, they stopped and fussed over him. James was again overjoyed by the positive attention his disguise inspired. So much so, that he almost forgot his purpose. Then, there they were, Abigail and Elizabeth and a group of girls, standing and talking, as if they hadn't a care in the world. This drove James onward. Soon they would care,

He walked towards them, determination written on his face, if that was possible. They never noticed that gleam in its eye, as they bent to fuss the white cat. Abigail was the first to speak, gushing over 'the gorgeous creature', claiming ownership of this 'marvellous' animal'. She picked James up roughly and held him above her head, like a prize she had won. Elizabeth grabbed at him, saying that no, the cat was hers. A tussle broke out and the girls snatched poor James from one to the other, arguing over who he belonged to. Memories filled his mind. This was just like those times when they had taunted him! This was not going to plan.

James began to get angry. He clawed at the grasping hands. Screams and shrieks rang out and suddenly he was dropped to the ground with a thud. He heard Abigail cry out,

"That horrible cat just scratched me." She pushed forward to show her hand where an ugly, red gash appeared across her knuckles.

"It scratched me too," shouted Elizabeth, her temper evidently rising. Her foot barely missed James' side as she lashed out. The girls began to raise their voices. Villagers looked on in horror. James scampered away, awaiting the next part of his plan.

It was not long before it began. The girls seeing him disappear around the side of the buildings, followed, ideas of 'getting that cat', filling their heads. James was pleased. He needed them to follow him to the alley at the side of the mill. His pace quickened, so did theirs. Soon the real scaring would begin. The girls followed James into the gloomy alleyway. The cat was now trapped, so they thought. It was a dead-end. James was filled with excitement. Revenge lay ahead. Abigail and Elizabeth signalled to the others to form a ring around the trapped cat. James tried to look frightened, arching his back, as he had seen other cats do. Elizabeth began to chant,

"Get the cat...Get the cat... Get the cat...!", the others joined in, filling the alley with a menacing noise.

They linked arms and began slowly to circle the cat, making sure their feet and legs barred any escape. James felt as if a prison wall was closing in on him. His eyes darted from face to face. Their expressions, as they stared at him, turning his blood cold. The chant quietened, until it was just a murmur, which itself was more menacing than their shouts. What would they try to do to him? Would he be able to put his plan into action before they started? Now, James was actually scared. The hackles at the back of his neck rose. He turned in the circle, baring his teeth and hissing. Their faces grew nearer, and their voices grew louder again. It was now or never. The piercing, ear-shattering roar, which emanated from James' mouth, could be heard all over the village.

Chapter Twelve

The Power of Magic

Immediately, as James anticipated, his cat became boy, still hissing and snarling at the circle of girls. Their faces once menacing, now reflected their horror. They drew back. Before they could completely grasp what had happened, James chanted the five simple words in a quiet, subdued tone: His once pale white hands gradually grew razor sharp claws. His innocent, pink eyes slanted, as silver gleaming whiskers positioned themselves around a black triangular nose. Pure, white fur covered his body, whilst he stooped on all fours and changed shape and size. Finally, a swirling, mesmerizing tail completed the transformation. And so, James performed this sorcery over and over again, until the girls' mouths opened in horror and this time THEIR screams could be heard throughout the village.

The close-knit circle, woven by James' tormentors, split into shattered pieces. Girls ran hither and thither, screaming, shouting, wailing at the tops of their voices. Their feet, once intertwined, unravelled, as their arms flew heavenward in outrage. The melee struck out towards the unsuspecting street, a jumble of limbs, shocked faces and raised voices. They ran shrieking, as if the devil, himself pursued them: Not a black stallion with pounding hooves, but a white cat with a terrifying secret.

James in cat form, eventually stood silent at the end of the street, watching the drama unfold. The girls streamed down the main street, headed by Abigail Williams and Elizabeth Parris, running as fast as their shaking legs would carry them. Their faces contorted into horror, their voices rising and falling, as they remembered what they had witnessed. The noise was deafening. James looked on, intrigued. What would happen next? He was soon to find out.

Out of the church came Reverend Parris, seeking the source of the terrible din which had invaded his quiet prayers. He scowled, as he stared across the street at the group of unruly girls, their raised voices and bizarre behaviour bringing a deep frown to his forehead. The group seeing him became like statues, still, dumbstruck. The screeching and wailing, which had brought onto the street a good number of the villagers, suddenly ceased and it became deathly quiet. The silence was deafening. The girls' faces were white and their eyes wild, as they returned the reverend's stare. Then in terrible slow motion, faces twitching, eyes rolling, they turned as one, raised their hands and pointed an accusing finger along the street, where James' cat-figure stood in the shadows. The villagers ignoring their silent accusation, looked on, wondering what the reverend would do, what punishment he would favour for this dreadful display. James looked on wondering too. Would they reveal his secret to the reverend? Would he believe them?

As Reverend Parris began to walk with purpose, across to the girls, the majority, becoming aware of the disturbance they had caused, suddenly became alert, bowed their heads and quietly disappeared into the side streets and houses of the village. They knew there would be a price to pay for their behaviour. Children were seen, not heard! The punishment would come later, for now they just slipped away. The thought of the cat-boy still echoed around their minds. All went, except Abigail and Elizabeth, who still stood fixed to the spot, eyes glazed, mouths struck open in an ugly, silent scream.

When he approached them, they began to mumble and murmur, repeating prayers and chants they had heard: A mixture of the reverend's teachings and the sayings of Tituba, the old, Caribbean servant. Their voices rose and fell as they constantly repeated anything they could think of to ward off the terrifying evil that was James Tyler. While that 'evil' looked on, the girls were gathered up by the revered and ushered into his house, still chanting in distracted chorus.   Doctor Griggs was called and the villagers waited on the street to see what had caused such ungodly behaviour. It seemed to be a lifetime of waiting for James until the Doctor and the Reverend came out of the house. The villagers ceased their quiet speculation and looked to the door as the two gentlemen emerged with looks of serious anxiety on their faces. What did they have to say?

Reverend Parris stepped forward, about to speak, but the doctor, patting his arm in a sympathetic gesture stopped him. Clearing his throat he looked at the small gathering and in a quiet, dignified voice announced: -

"It seems brothers and sisters, we have witnessed today in these girls in this very street, an example of the power of witchcraft."

The crowd gasped and James...

Well, he wondered, in a numbed silence if he would be hanged!

Chapter Thirteen

The Web of Lies

Hanged! James knew this could be his fate, if the girls blamed their bizarre behaviour on him. He had heard that witchcraft, a few years ago, had been deemed to be against the law by their English governors. Others before him had been hanged. If he was accused, then who knew what would follow? The problem had to be solved, his mistake rectified. Think. He must seek out Abigail and Elizabeth and somehow deter them from revealing more of what they had seen; Stop them accusing him. But how? They had surely been scared by his transformation, but could he scare them into keeping silent? Whatever he did, it needed to be done quickly.

James returned to the barn to think. Had he been stupid? Had he made things worse? Indecision kept his mind tied in knots and he was unable to unravel a plan to put right his wrong doing. However, he could not regret his motives nor his action, but the outcome, well that was something he had not been able to control. What to do? Perhaps he should find the girls and scare them into keeping quiet, perhaps suggest another to blame? This sparked a small flame in James' mind. Thoughts rolled out one after another; Threaten them;   Give them someone else to blame; Persuade them; Put ideas into their heads;   Plead innocence;   Name another;   Not my fault! Accuse someone else; Find a plausible substitute.   Images, ideas and scenarios gusted round and around in his head. Questions led to more questions: Who? How? Why? Who could he accuse? Someone who had a history; someone the girls knew well; someone who was not like the others; someone suspicious; Tituba!

Once the name popped into his head, James knew that this was the very person he must accuse. Not openly, but secretly to be acknowledged only by Abigail or Elizabeth. No thought came to him about what fate might befall Tituba, he thought only to free himself from this terrible situation. His mind made up, he strolled back into the village, his usual self. All the way there, he rehearsed in his head what he would do. As he reached the main street, all was quiet. The villagers had retired behind closed doors to talk in hushed whispers about the doctor's earlier announcement.   James clutched the cat pendant, convincing himself that this was what he needed to do. With purpose, he marched down the main street towards the church. He must find Elizabeth. He must tell her his 'truth' and she MUST believe him!

It was surprisingly easy to locate her: She stood wide-eyed and ashen faced at the window of her house, next to the church. As James peered in, he could see that she was alone. He had chosen Elizabeth because she was younger, less sure of herself than Abigail. Realising that this would be to his advantage, Elizabeth was his prey today. Moving towards the window, he raised the hand holding the pendant and reflected its light onto Elizabeth's stricken face. Temporarily blinded, she gasped and peered harder out of the window. At that moment, James dropped the pendant and stepped into full view.

"Elizabeth," he whispered. "Don't scream... I have come to explain everything."

"Is that you, James Tyler?" Elizabeth retorted in shocked anguish.

"It is I," James answered. "Don't be afraid. I will explain everything. That dreadful show in the alley was not my fault." James forced his voice to tremble, while he stood almost smiling, his face turned away from Elizabeth.

"It is NOT my fault, Elizabeth. Please believe me, I..." James stalled for effect. "I have been bewitched from my birth. If you allow, I will explain and then you will see that this is not of my doing!"

Elizabeth persuaded but still frightened, nodded her head and signalled for James to draw closer. James smiled.

Perhaps he would be saved after all. Hanged? Not him. He smiled again,

Chapter Fourteen

The Alliance of Elizabeth Parris

Relief flooded through James. Elizabeth was at least prepared to listen. He would have to convince her, talk the talk, and then she would persuade Abigail and the others that this was not his fault. It was so simple. Staring at Elizabeth, he realized that his life depended on her belief: Depended upon his ability to lie convincingly. He stopped, never had dso much depended on his powers of persuasion. Lying did not come easily to James, the son of the devout Mrs Tyler. He imagined his mother's voice whispering her wise council in his ear:-

"Do not EVER lie, James Tyler. God hears. God punishes. God lets the truth be known!" This flashed- back to him from long ago, accompanied by a sharp twinge in his hands, where they had been struck with a stick to accompany this dire warning. If he lied, would God strike him dead, was his mother right? Surely God was more forgiving? Whatever the outcome, what alternative did he have? Whatever he did, his fate was sealed. He had to risk it, the hangman's noose beckoned. James was scared. Lie he must or die at the hands of the witch's hangman! It would take just one accusation.

At that moment, Elizabeth's shaky voice interrupted his reverie.

"The truth, James Tyler.   Tell me the truth," she breathed.   Her face was still tinged with grey and her hands still trembled.   Running through her head was an image of James Tyler changing from cat to boy and back again: Such a beautiful cat, such an ugly boy! James took a deep breath and plunged headlong into a web of lies.

"You see my appearance, Elizabeth; well that is part of an enchantment.   I am like this because the witches of this village made me this way.   I was born colourless and destined to transform into a cat at their command."   There it was said... the lie! "My mother, well she hates me because she knows the truth and she cannot live with it, she cannot change it.   So every day I pay dearly for the witches' curse."   James savoured the pathetic ring to his words which added credence to his lie. And Elizabeth... well she took it all in and believed every word. She listened silently as James lamented his fate at the hands of these hateful, hated creatures of darkness, never once named, never once revealed, but always accused.   These ghostly beings, the witches were damned by James' words, damned by their imagined actions and totally, believingly real to the frightened, confused Elizabeth.   Her already pale face, paled further as James revealed the terror of his unendurable life at the hands of these invented tormentors, who controlled his pathetic body and turned it when they would from cat to boy and from boy to cat.

Elizabeth believed with every fibre of her body. Shock stung like a thousand bees at James' words. Disgust and hatred changed to sympathy, as she imagined his terrible, terrifying life. Her imagination ran wild. She saw James stricken by his afflicted appearance, ridiculed and excluded by his family and the villagers. Finally, she imagined the horror of all horrors, the added terror of never knowing whether he was cat or human. How confused and unloved he must feel. Her earlier tormenting lay forgotten, as she placed herself firmly in his shoes. James sighed and whimpered and hung his head... to hide the victorious sparkle in his eyes. Wicked boy!

"Your life must be dreadful, James. What can I do to help?" she said pityingly, at that moment ready to promise him anything. James smiled and whimpered once more for effect. He had won her over. She would say whatever he wanted her to say. A great rush of power washed over him and for just that instant he imagined the world was his. Wicked, wicked boy.

The following Sunday, the last in January, in church, James sat quietly next to his parents, like on every other Sunday. The Reverend Parris droned on through an interminably long sermon, which James had not heard the half of. Everyone was there. James had half expected reference to the events of the previous week, but all were silent. Having paid attention initially, his mind now began to wander, as did his eyes around the room. He smiled secretly as he spied Betty Parris and Abigail Williams, crouching subdued in their pew. Wicked thoughts filled his head. What if? What if he reinforced their fear and their sympathy?

Everyone so intent on the reverend's strong sermon did not notice James' silently slip out of the church where he transformed into Snowflake. He then crept back through the door and down the church until he reached the girls. He brushed silently against their legs and made a small cat whimper. Immediately the reverends' daughter stood, screamed and fell into a fit on the floor. Witches were here. Other girls, seeing the cat followed suit, causing a great commotion in the once quiet church. One of the girls, with thoughts of scaring off the white cat and the fear of witches, barked like a dog whilst another flapped her arms to shoo him away. James smiled, and concealing himself behind a pillar, quietly meowed and became himself again, just in time for his mother to gather him up with his sister and rush them home as fast as they could walk.

Chapter Fifteen

A Judgement is Confirmed

It was February and a few weeks had passed since the villagers had witnessed the bizarre behaviour of the girls in the street and the church. James continued to feed his lies, his 'truth' to Elizabeth, who hung on to every word, believed every carefully constructed untruth. He had not yet revealed the instigator of this alleged witchcraft, but waited, knowing that Elizabeth was poised ready, passing on, embroidering the tale of magic and sorcery. He knew by the way Abigail and the others looked at him, not with hatred but with a kind of grudging sympathy and yes he decided, awe! He had attained cult status in the eyes of his once tormentors. He bathed in it.

But now time was running out and it would be prudent, he thought, to deliver the final blow and reveal the name. Walking with more confidence and it seemed a good bit taller, James set off for the village to alert Elizabeth to the final piece of the puzzle. He had no need, since the escapade in church, to use the spell, to change. No-one bothered with him anymore. It was as if they all ignored his appearance, forgot. Even his family seemed preoccupied. Blithely following his plan, James was unaware of the great storm, which was brewing in the village, set in motion by that one ill-advised act of defiance and revenge . He walked on. Should he accuse Tituba of witchcraft? Would it achieve anything? Did anyone care anymore?

There had been no comeback whatsoever from his cat changes. He had spoon-fed the lies to Elizabeth, who had dutifully passed them on. #That was as far as it went. No obvious punishment had been meted out to the girls. Their behaviour had not been questioned or even mentioned in church or in any public place. Did he need to accuse anyone? Or was it all forgotten?

As he walked up the main street, James could see a crowd of villagers gathering outside the church. There was a sort of hushed expectancy emanating from the group, as if they were preparing to hear important news. At the far side, he saw his own mother and father and wondered in a distracted sort of way, why this meeting had been called. His mother and father rarely came to the church together, except on Sundays and this was definitely not Sunday! Watching carefully, James saw Abigail and Elizabeth and the other girls paraded out in front of the church, their heads hung low. They wore their Sunday best clothes, dressed for an important occasion. Was this the punishment? Was this the time that he was accused? A distorted image of the hangman's noose flashed through his mind.

Behind the girls, Reverend Parris and Doctor Griggs shuffled from one foot to the other, presenting austere faces to the crowd. A wave of expectant whispers ushered its way through the gathering, as they saw the two serious, adult faces. James knew they were here to pronounce judgement on the events in January.

Chapter Sixteen

The First Witch Accused

Before it was too late, James knew he must name names, now so that only Elizabeth could hear. Doctor Griggs moved forward, as James searched through his brain for ideas, a plan. How could he tell Elizabeth without anyone else hearing? The doctor cleared his throat, as he always did, and began to speak in a grave tone.

"Brothers and Sisters, following the strange behaviour exhibited by these girls," he said, as he turned and acknowledged them, "the reverend and I have made clear and thorough investigation into the cause. We feel obliged to point out that these girls are not in any way to blame for the said behaviour and we confirm our original opinion that their unusual display was the result of unlawful witchcraft." Nodding, the villagers agreed with the pronouncement. Beyond shock, expecting this conclusion, James now understood the preoccupation that seemed to have invaded the village. What should he do? He could feel the hangman's noose around his neck. What if Abigail and Elizabeth accused him?

An idea flashed through his head. He could do it. He had to. Everything depended on his success. As the doctor continued, mentioning similar happenings four years previously, James quickly hid and turned himself into the cat. He listened as the doctor sited the case of the Goodwin children who had demonstrated behaviour like that of the girls. James moved slowly through the legs of the crowd, keeping his eyes firmly on the faces of Elizabeth and Abigail. The doctor continued,

"Of course we will all recall that Goody Glover was hanged for witchcraft after these incidents, despite Reverend Cotton Mather's attempts to persuade her to repent. We will also recall that poor Martha Goodwin never recovered and to this day is still bewitched!" Gasps and sighs of remembrance and pity washed through the crowd.

"We must now hope that these poor children are not to be stricken in the same way." The reverend swept his hand across to where those poor children stood. The crowd murmured their agreement.

James heard all this, as he relentlessly moved through the sea of legs towards his goal. The reverend and the doctor were bound to ask the question now, bound to seek a name. Please God, let it not be his. The noose tightened. At last, James reached his target. Elizabeth saw him, recognized him and her mouth fell open. Was she going to scream? Point an accusing finger? Quickly, James scratched with his claws in the dust, willing Elizabeth to see and understand. He could not risk anyone else seeing, so he just as speedily scraped over the dusty word. The reverend was now whipping up a storm, calling to God to help reveal the name of the wicked sorcerer. The adults in the street, now frenzied, raised their voices, calling for blood! When had the atmosphere changed? When had the fire and brimstone approach begun? When had Reverend Parris taken over?

As James, now hiding, silently changed back to boy, the reverend took an almighty breath, raised his arms heavenward and screeched the dreaded question.
"It is now your God-given duty, my poor children to make your accusation; To name the evil one: Who is the witch?" he demanded, squaring an unnerving eye on the girls. The gathering stood motionless; eyes fixed on the girls' faces.

"Who is the witch?" The reverends voice rang out in q mighty doom-laden bellow.
James held his breath. Let my name not pass their lips. Please God!
The crowd waited, the reverend screamed,

"Who is the WITCH?" He pointed a finger directly at his daughter, who paled, looked down at the dusty floor, then raised her head, eyes wide and in a clear bell-like voice replied.

"Tituba." And in an instant the imagined noose fell to the ground with a shuddering thud.

Chapter Seventeen

The Witch Hunt

And so it began; the witch hunt of Salem. The crowd unsurprised by the name, turned to each other and damned Tituba with every word and expression.

"I knew it," shouted one man, as another strode out with purpose towards the place where he knew he would find the accused. Others followed their dignity and staidness forgotten, as they struck out to capture the offender. Poor Tituba, poor innocent Tituba sat at home, unaware of her fate, which had been determined by a cat and bullied child.

The angry, unforgiving crowd collected in an untidy rabble at the door of the reverend's house where Tituba was enslaved. The reverend and the doctor followed quickly at their heels, calming, cajoling, trying to diffuse the situation, they had themselves caused. The gathered people of Salem motioned with every hand, every voice for Tituba to be dragged from the house and hanged forthwith. The doctor and the reverend, regretting what they had unwittingly started, spoke quietly but with firmness and despite their frenzy the crowd began to take notice of their voices. Years of teaching and duty falling back on their shoulders, their faces recently twisted in hatred becoming bland as they listened to the calming tones of the reverend's voice.

"Brothers, Sisters," he began, as he scrutinized their blank faces. "We shall not be hasty in our accusation and punishment. We must follow the law and if Tituba is innocent, then she will be saved. But if she is found guilty... by God, then she will be punished as written in the law."

The people knew the wisdom of the reverend's words. Had they not listened, believed, and followed his teaching this last three years. They trusted his judgment; justice would be done. They began to drift away, nodding knowingly at each other, and in the direction of the reverend and the doctor, who breathed in relief at their departure. Still inside, Tituba sat unconcerned, unaware of the commotion in the street outside the house. Would she have run away, if she had known? Even she knew that once accused the end was inevitable. Even she knew the impossibility of the situation. If she had known perhaps, she would have slipped away in the night before the magistrate banged on the door.

James stood staring at that very door. He had been caught up in the crowd as they had driven relentlessly towards this house. Mixed emotions gnawed at James' soul, relief, excitement, guilt, remorse. Should he tell Tituba, warn her of what had happened? Dare he? If he did, would Elizabeth then accuse him? He dared not risk it, so he took one last look at the house where Tituba dwelt, unsuspecting of her fate, then sidled away and disappeared into the fading light. He walked home, his fingers clenching and unclenching at his side. What had he done? He was aware of what would almost certainly happen to Tituba. Poor innocent Tituba, whose fate had been determined by his actions. What had he done?

Chapter Eighteen

More Accused and Arrested

The next day, a very subdued Elizabeth Parris was taken to the magistrate where she formally accused Tituba of witchcraft. Abigail Williams, her cousin and her family were also there, and she backed up Elizabeth's story. Neither girl saw fit to site James Tyler in the accusation: Both imagining him a victim not a perpetrator, who had suffered enough at the witch's hands. As they accused Tituba, saying they had seen her watching them before their strange behaviour began, little did they care that she had no direct connection with their display and that they had only James' word that she had bewitched him. Such a convincing story James had woven, that thoughts of not believing him never entered their empty heads. They told the magistrate how Tituba had told stories of witchcraft and had shown them magic from her native home in Barbados. Dark magic from a dark and mysterious land. She had read their fortunes and promised them all kinds of sorcery. Play and toys not allowed in their strict upbringing, their evenings had been spent instead, around the kitchen fire, whilst Tituba had filled their heads with witchcraft.

Their description of the dark side of the world shocked those around them to the core. Later, the two girls were joined by others who had also taken part in Tituba's forbidden evenings, and it soon became clear that there were others to be accused. The girls, frightened that they would be punished, grasped at any name, any villager who might be imagined a witch. The group mentioned Sarah Good and Sarah Osborne and the magistrate duly recorded their names under the heading 'The Accused Witches of Salem'.

That evening, arrest warrants were issued and the three women were all taken into custody. They were to be examined by magistrates, John Hathorne and Jonathan Corwin and from then their fate was never to be in doubt. Tituba was taken from the reverend's house and as she was marched unceremoniously down the main street, held tightly on both sides by the magistrates, in full hearing of the whole village, attested her guilt in a deep, caustic voice: Claiming her magic would save her, that no-one could hold her down for long. She screamed, she shouted, reciting dark magic, as she gloried in her power. The other two women came more slowly, quietly to their examination, both vehemently denying the accusation in whispered voices: Such gentle, unassuming souls, but outcasts because of their unusual lifestyles. No-one believed them. No-one cared enough.

Hysteria took hold of every man, woman and child in Salem: Their only thoughts to rid the town of witches. Tituba's confession was held up to the village as proof of their concern. On later examination evidence of her magic was revealed to all who would listen. How she made 'witch cake' and fed it to a stray dog, to counteract the spell on poor Betty Parris and her cousin Abigail. The stray dog was named as Tituba's link with the devil. Everyone knew that dogs were the devil's familiar. Tituba was damned by the population and the two other women were damned alongside her. The three were carted off to prison to await formal trial, but the frenzy; the hysteria did not stop there.

And as for James, he just stood by, watching, listening, filled with anguish and guilt at what he had started: No longer afraid of the hangman's noose, but of a greater retribution. His mother's words rang out like a death knell through his mind, deep down to his soul:-

"Do not EVER lie, James Tyler. God hears. God punishes.   God lets the truth be known!"

When would God punish him? How would it happen? JHe knew that it was inevitable; his mother had told him so time after time. His misery was deeper than any he had experienced before. Great sobs racked his body at night; dry- eyed horror haunted his days. He could not undo what he had done. He could not right his terrible wrong. He could not stop this hunt. He truly was the devil's work, just as his mother had said.

Chapter Nineteen

The Box Buried, a Witch Dies

In the days which followed, a strange sort of truce grew gradually between James and his mother. He had taken to praying more frequently, carrying out his chores more diligently and he always, always did exactly as he was told. In return, his mother treated him with a little more kindness, not gently but with more tolerance. Calm befell the Tyler household. However, James could not take advantage of this newfound acceptance because he had exchanged one misery for another. He was now not punished by his parents, but constantly berated himself for the devastating damage he had caused. Therefore, trying to recompense, James decided that the spell should never be used again and he planned to return it to the wood.

One bright afternoon in early June, after his chores had been carefully done, James took the spell book and pendant and set off at speed to the woods. This was better done quickly and without thought. He easily found the tree and the spot in the woods where he had uncovered the spell book. The ground still looked newly disturbed to James' eye, even though it must surely have been battered by rain and wind over the last months. There were no spring flowers growing here, just bare earth. James scratched at that surface then pushed great clumps of earth aside and soon a deep chasm of a hole had been dug and the box revealed. Without thought, without regret he placed the book and pendant into the box and buried it again. About to leave, he looked back and seeing the earth so newly disturbed, he decided to place some nearby stones and boulders over the top, to deter others from finding this devil's book.

A job satisfactorily done, James set off, no spring in his step this time, but some small part of his sadness lifting from his heart. At least no-one else, including himself, would be able to use the spell again. This would have to suffice. On his way home, he followed a route which took him through the village. This place held no fear for him now. No-one bothered with him. They were too caught up in a mounting witch hunt. James deliberately went by the mill, where he hoped he might hear news. He had developed a morbid sort of curiosity, which persuaded him to follow the witch hunt to its bitter end. What news would he hear today? So many of the villagers, his neighbours and family friends, had been trapped in this madness. He counted in his head. He reckoned well over a hundred people had been accused and imprisoned awaiting trial, including poor Dorcan Good, who was only four years old.

What had he started? When would it end? Was this constant guilt his punishment?

A sudden movement caught James' eye. As he looked towards the mill door, a man was rushing through it, muttering to himself. After he had entered, James could hear a quiet commotion inside, whispered gasps and hushed surprise. What had the man said? While he wondered as to the cause of the fuss, the man emerged from the shop, looked directly at him and said,

"Have you heard the news, boy?" James looked at the stricken face of the man.

"No, sir. What is the news?" James replied, not really anticipating anything which would interest him.

The man's eyes looked around, calling at passing villagers to come and hear his fascinating news. A small crowd gathered around James, waiting. The man looked around again, assuring himself that there were enough people there to appreciate his announcement.

"I've just come from the trial of Bridget Bishop," he announced. James knew that name. It was the woman from the farm next to his. She had been dragged away in the middle of the night and, as he found out later, accused of being a witch: One more poor soul to blame him.

"Well!" exclaimed a woman in the crowd. "Tell us what happened." Others murmured their interest and James moved closer to catch the news.

The man looked around the mass of faces. This was his chance, he had a captive audience. He would play out the scene in its full glory.

"Bridget Bishop has been tried for witchcraft." he started.

"We know that!" the crowd was becoming restless.

"Get on with it, Brother, do!" encouraged an impatient looking woman.

"Well," confided the man. "The evidence which was given in court was so awful, I could not listen to it. The terrible things she has done. The poor victims..." He paused, drawing out the story, ready to deliver the one bit of real news he had. He drew breath ready to continue to describe these crimes, but the gathering started to turn away, to find someone else, who would just tell them what had happened. The man, seeing his opportunity drifting away, rushed on:-

"GUILTY!" he shouted. "Guilty as charged. The first of many, I reckon!"

The crowd turned back.

"And..." an anxious voice uttered. James looked to the woman who had spoken. It was Bridget Bishop's best friend... His own mother.

"Sentenced to death by hanging," the man relished the final word. The crowd gasped, then quickly recovered, nodding their support of the verdict.

James watched as the crowd dispersed, leaving his mother stark and alone in the street. Her face looked gaunt, and a slight twitch had appeared at the corner of her eye. She said nothing. James then, for the first time in his life, took his mother's hand and led her safely home.

Chapter Twenty

A Final Accusation

From that day forth his mother rarely spoke a word. She prayed in absolute silence and never once reminded James and her family of their duty, as she had done so many times in the past. Accusations were rife in the town. Abigail, Elizabeth and the others continued to point the finger at whomsoever they chose enjoying their fame. Other villagers made accusations too, some to save themselves from the hangman's noose. And Bridget Bishop... Well on a fine day, June 10th to be exact, she was hanged on Gallows' Hill in full view of Salem's finest. Never once did she scream, never once did she deny the accusation, but prayed only to God for his forgiveness. The villagers and nearby townspeople were shocked by her lack of vehemence, so much so that Nathaniel Saltonstall, doubting the validity of the verdict, resigned from the court that day.

Then one quiet, eerie night, there came a great banging at James' door. He and his family were sat eating a late supper in uncomfortable silence, when a familiar voice demanded:-
"Open up, Brother Tyler. We have urgent business to attend to!"

James' father cast his eyes around his family, real fear appearing for the first time as his gaze settled on James. The banging and demands continued as each of the Tylers in turn faced the other with questioning eyes. Who were they here for? They all knew that the voice outside their door belonged to Brother Corwin, Nathanial Saltonstall's replacement.

In slow motion it seemed, Mr Tyler took one last longing look at his family and rose to open the door. He knew, as did the others, once cornered, there was no escape. The door was pulled back with a reluctant, anguished squeak, to reveal Corwin and his fellow magistrates standing, lamp-lit at the door. "Brother Tyler," Corwin began. "We have today taken statement from one of the villagers that you are harbouring witches in your household. They had not come just for him then.

"We demand to come in and to take for trial the witches you have here." He continued. Were all three of them to be accused? James froze. Suely he deserved this, but his mother and his sister Rebecca, did they?

Corwin produced a paper which told of the arrest of those who stood accused. Unrolling the document, he showed James' father, then moved to the table where the others sat, still, dumbstruck, not ready for the inevitable.

The magistrate stood tall, with authority and ignoring James, spoke only to the two other occupants of the table.

"It is my duty to arrest you, Mary Tyler and you, Rebecca Tyler for the crime of witchcraft. Have you anything to say in your defence?"

Both stared in horror as their names passed their accuser's lips. When he had finished, Rebecca stood, clasped a hand over her mouth, and casting stricken eyes towards her father, pleaded for his denial. None came. James' mother continued to sit at the table, as if cast from stone, no expression on her face. Rebecca, finding no support, began to scream, wailing her innocence, pleading, saying some mistake must have been made. Mrs Tyler just sat, the twitch at her eye, now making its appearance. James' heart missed a beat, then thumped in his chest, as if it would explode.

Should he defend them, should he confess all? He knew for certain that this would not save them. They may only escape if they accused another. Accuse me, he willed, accuse me, his mind screamed out to them. I surely deserve it. But neither his mother nor his sister even looked in his direction. So it was to be as it was now. Two strong-looking men gathered up Rebecca's screaming, rejecting body and moved, dragging her across to the door. Two others made their way towards the silent Mrs Tyler. As they drew near, Corwin slid his body in front of them to ask:-

"Have you nothing to say, before you are taken away, Mary Tyler."

Mrs Tyler's eyes never once wavered as she raised them and pinned Brother Corwin's eyes with her own.

"May God forgive you." she breathed quietly, as she rose and without assistance and with great dignity walked towards the door.

The men swiftly removed themselves and their prisoners through the door, closing it with a click behind them. James' overriding memory of that night, the one that haunted his dreams for the rest of his life, was the sight of heartfelt pity on the face of the magistrate, as he looked back from the door...And the journey of one large teardrop, as it forged its way down his father's colourless face.

Chapter Twenty-One

The Day of the Trial

In the next few days, James knew what real punishment felt like. Not the seeming rejection by his parents, not the tormenting of his peers, but the knowledge that his doing had broken his family apart. His mother and sister lay accused in jail, his father at home trapped in his own self-made prison. James riddled with guilt and unable to change what he had started, worked hard at his chores, prayed hard for his family and asked God that the punishment should be his and that this culling of innocent people might stop. Stop now. But the hysteria continued, more innocents died by the noose or were lying in jail. Within days he and his father learned that Mrs Tyler was to be tried the next week. Of his sister, Rebecca, they heard nothing.

On the day of the trial, James' father insisted that they both wear their best church clothes, that his wife would expect no less. James dressed carefully but with little stomach for what was to come. They arrived early at the courthouse and sat where they would be able to see both the accused and the judge. James sat still, heart beating, wishing that somehow his mother would find it within herself to accuse him, the devil child, the one who was different. To accuse another, would release her. Lost in his thoughts, he was not prepared for the start of proceedings however. Mrs Tyler was brought into court; hands tied behind her back, clothes ragged and dirty, great black streaks marring her face. Her eyes dulled and beaten, head low, she stood in the dock a defeated woman.

As she entered the court great jeers rose filling the room. Violent, scathing comments filled the air.

"Wicked witch."

"Devils' spawn."

"Killer sorceress."

Vile names, spoken in vitriolic tones rang out around the room, until James, unable to bear it any longer, covered his ears with unsteady hands. Then to his surprise his father with gentle hands, removed them from his ears and whispered,

"They are wrong, James." It was the first time his father had spoken to him in years. They were the first words he had uttered in defence of his wife.

The trial began. A list of accusers and crimes were read. James listened as circumstantial evidence was paraded before the judge: All hard to prove but nevertheless damning. Then, James became aware of eyes upon him, as he, himself was sited as proof of Mary Tyler's guilt. Words he had heard his mother say in private were repeated in the court. How she believed that James was a punishment for her wrongdoing. This wrongdoing was interpreted as witchcraft. James stood abruptly, to deny what they were saying. but again the gentle hands of his father, pulled him back to his seat. As James looked at his father a wan smile passed his lips and his head shook.

"I do not want to lose you too, son" he said. This was the first time that he had been acknowledged as such.

James was too frightened for his mother to appreciate this strange change of attitude: Nevertheless, a small part of his being treasured that moment. The courtroom listened on as more lies and embroidered truths were told. The final blow came, when it was pointed out that Mary Tyler and Bridget Bishop were best friends, always together, working at each other's house.

"Surely this is proof in itself", the judge was told. "Together the two women plotted against the god-fearing folk of Salem." Bridget Bishop had already been tried and hanged. What further proof did they need?

Great shouts of guilty rang out around the room. Not one man or woman spoke up for poor Mary Tyler. James knew how that felt. He could feel his father's body tense as the judge called for order, ready for his pronouncement. James knew, before the judge uttered a word what the outcome would be. His punishment demanded it.

"Mary Tyler," the judge began. "I find you guilty on all charges of witchcraft. And I sentence you to be hanged on Gallows' Hill as soon as this can be arranged. The judge's voice was solemn and to the point. Cheers and whoops of agreement spread through the court and into the streets. Those less exuberant nodded their agreement. James and his father sat shocked...

Then Mary Tyler suddenly looked at her son's stricken face and to his amazement her eyes once dulled, lit with the light of battle and promised that this would not end here. James knew that look. He had glimpsed it in her eyes before, unnoticed, when the village people talked about his shortcomings.

Chapter Twenty-Two

Escape but Not Perfect

On the day of execution, James awoke at first light with a plan formed inside his head. He had lain awake half the night thinking, plotting, planning until eventually he had dozed just before dawn. Once dressed, he moved to the door ready to put his plan into action. Thinking ahead, he first carried out his chores, so that his father would not think that he was up to no good. Those finished, he scuttled off to the woods. Although he had said he would never use the spell again, this time he promised himself it would be different. This time it would be used to undo part of the mayhem he had so unwittingly started. He ran as fast as his legs would go. The hanging was due to take place at noon. He must be ready before then.

After he reached the stone-marked spot, without delay, he pushed aside the stones and boulders, dug away the earth and retrieved the box, the book, and the pendant. He then returned to the house, long before his father might have noticed he was missing. At home, having greeted his father, he secreted himself in the barn, to finally run through his plan. The box and book were left hidden in a sack and the pendant firmly placed around his neck for when next James left the barn. He knew where his mother and sister were being held of course, but he needed cunning and a certain amount of luck to execute their release. It would not be simple, but he did have some immensely powerful magic to aid him. The irony of the situation did not make him smile.

The jail was dirty and full of the accused. A lone guard, held the keys and the lives of the prisoners in his hands. James knew he must steal the keys, release his mother and sister and return the keys, all before they came to take his mother away. First, he hid and changed into his white cat, then he went looking for the guard. He found him sat at his table, reading his bible in hushed tones. What should he do? How could he steal the keys? He saw them hanging from the belt of the guard and knew that he would need to be in boy form to unhook them. The plan was not to go exactly as he thought. How could he just walk up to the guard and take the keys? This was impossible.

Then a flash of inspiration hit him square. He did not need to be a boy. He could do this as Snowflake! Sauntering towards the guard, James oozed feigned confidence. As before, with the girls and the villagers, the guard was smitten with the beautiful, white cat. Perhaps this was part of the magic.

"Come on puss," he cooed. "Come see me. It is not often we see things of beauty in this place!"

James strolled towards the guard, his eyes firmly fixed on the keys. As he neared, the guard moved and the keys jangled at his side. This was James' opportunity. Like any cat alerted to a strange noise, James eyes were drawn further towards the keys. He stretched out his paw and tapped them to repeat the sound. So far, so good, the guard did not object to that.

"Like my keys, do you puss? Like the sound?" The guard smiled, amused by this simple game. He jostled the keys at his waist one more time, but the sound was dampened as they clunked against his side.

Thinking nothing more than of the game, the guard removed the keys and jangled them in front of James, who returned the favour by pawing at them. So this simple, desperate game proceeded, until James was sure that he had established a friend. Then as James reached once more for the keys, he allowed his claws to slide out and with planned thought he thrust into the hand of the guard. Knowing that he had to make a good job of the damage, James clawed again and the guard jumped back with a cry of pain. Blood spilled from the scratches and dripped to the floor. The guard tossed the keys at the table and ran from the room to see to his bleeding hand. Immediately James retrieved the keys and raced with them to where he knew that his mother and sister were being held. It was as well he had found this out on his arrival, because there would surely not have been enough time to search now.

Finding Rebecca alone in the cell, James was temporarily stopped in his tracks. Where was his mother? Not enough time to consider that now, he weaved his body through the bars of the cell and dropped the keys at his sister's feet. Stunned at the sight of her cat, Rebecca at first did not register the keys in front of her. James scraped at them to alert her. Understanding immediately, Rebecca picked them up, unlocked the cell, squeezed through the door and locked it again. What should she do now? Snowflake was at her feet, clawing for the keys. She dropped them and the cat snatched them up in its mouth and disappeared. Rebecca fled out of the prison with more haste than grace and hid.

James returned the keys and disappeared just as the guard returned to his table, a white handkerchief strapped around his hand. Thinking the cat had taken fright, he attached the keys back onto his belt and continued the interrupted read of his bible. Before James went in search of Rebecca, he quickly reversed the spell. As he did so, he saw his mother being led away by two armed guards. There was little he could do for her now. He found Rebecca, not far away, hiding behind a wall, where she was carefully looking out for the guard. James tapped her gently on the shoulder and when she turned, terrified, he smiled, placed a finger over his lips and pointed in the direction of their house. They both made the journey home in silence, until they reached the bolt hole in the barn.

"How did you do that?" Rebecca whispered. "How did you get Snowflake to do that? James smiled. How indeed? Rebecca would be shocked when she found out.

Chapter Twenty-Three

A Different Transformation

Rebecca had seen too, as her mother had been led away. Anguish gnawed at both their hearts. Forgetting her earlier question, she asked James another.

"What can we do to help mother?"

James had no other plan.

"I think there is nothing we can do, Rebecca. I came for both of you, but there was not enough time." His voice was deep with regret and remorse, as he hung his head in defeat.

"Perhaps if we go to the hill, we can save her there," she suggested, smiling brightly to encourage her brother. James doubted that but was prepared to try anything.

"But, Rebecca, we both cannot go. If you are seen, the magistrate will arrest you again and they will use it as proof of your guilt," James pointed out.

"You cannot do it alone, James Tyler!" Rebecca's tone reminded him of his mother. "I will hide, disguise myself and we WILL go together."

Suddenly, miraculously an idea sprang into James' head: The spell, they could use the spell again, but this time on Rebecca. He had no idea whether it would work, but it was worth a try.

Whether they could then save their mother was another doubt, but they must try this too. For the next few minutes, James spun the tale of the spell book and pendant to an unbelieving Rebecca. He took the book from its hiding place, pulled out the pendant from around his neck and showed them to her. He did not tell her how he had used this spell, for fear she would turn against him.

"How do you think Snowflake brought you the keys?" he questioned Rebecca. "Because Snowflake is me." He answered his own question. Rebecca was still doubtful.

"Have you ever seen Snowflake and I together? No, you have not. Admit it. Because Snowflake is me!" he almost screamed the words.

"Oh, I think perhaps then I had better show you." And with that promise, James said the five words and the proof stood right in front of Rebecca. She looked aghast at his transformation. She asked herself if she should run, should she scream, should she accuse her brother of witchcraft? That thought stopped the questions. It was witchcraft that had brought them to this: Their mother's innocence for such a crime.

"Turn back, James!" she demanded. "Turn back and we will talk."

Without ceremony, James became av boy again. They talked more of what they could do. They made plans, but soon it was time for them to try the spell on Rebecca. Noon drew near. They must be at the hill in time if they were to save their mother. James carefully placed the pendant around his sister's neck and told her the words she must say. Nervously Rebecca ran the words through her memory. Did she want to risk this? What if she was turned into something else? What if she was transported away, trapped forever?

"Just do it, please Rebecca. I had those doubts too. Just trust that it will work. Please..."

Within seconds of Rebecca whispering the words, the magic began. James now understood the reaction of the girls when he had first changed. It was incredible, frightening, exciting! Before his eyes, Rebecca's face grew transparent whiskers grew and her eyes slanted into emerald beauty. Her hair rolled up and in and two perfect brown ears appeared. She gracefully bent, as her shape and size changed. And most astounding of all, the colour of her skin changed through tawny shades to eventually settle into the most beautiful tortoiseshell coat. The transformation was mesmerizing.

James roused himself. There was no time to waste. Calling Rebecca to follow him, they both set off at pace to Gallows' Hill.

Would they save their mother? Who was to know? They would try very hard; they would try everything within their power and understanding. James sent up a silent prayer. It was a prayer of regret, remorse, and hope.

Chapter Twenty-Four

Gallows' Hill

When James and Rebecca arrived at Gallows' Hill, a silent and sombre crowd had gathered to watch the proceedings. They both marvelled at the fascination these staid people had developed for the ceremonious murder of one of their own. What nonsense was in their heads to even contemplate this? James found a place next to his father and Rebecca, disguised, sat close. The two Tyler children had not come with any set plan, they had a vague notion of distracting the crowd, so that James could release his mother, but this seemed an impossible task now. Maybe in their heart of hearts they knew that they were here to witness their mother's execution. Misery settled around their hearts.

A drum roll alerted the crowd to the arrival of Mary Tyler. She had sent home for a crisply laundered dress and bonnet, which she had donned with dignity and pride. One of the prison guards had allowed her to wash her dirty face and her skin shone with cleanliness. On the wooden platform of the gallows, she stood proud like the great oak, nobility shining out from every fibre of her being. Her eyes were lit by an inner strength, an inner belief in God. Anyone who was not blinded by the hysteria of the moment could see that this woman was innocent!

Mr Tyler suddenly noticing James by his side, squeezed his hand and whispered.

"Rebecca will be saved, son. I promise you that," James nodded, already knowing the reality of that fact.

"Your mother will not die in vain. We will beat this terrible disease that invades our village, James. No-one else will die innocently." James' father said each word with such conviction that James believed implicitly. He could feel burning tears imprisoned behind his eyes, waiting to be released. He could feel the tense body of the cat, his sister at his feet. They both had given up hope and accepted the inevitable.

The drum roll came again, and James watched as the noose he had imagined around his own neck, was lifted and place around that of his mother. He almost stepped forward at that moment, confession weighing heavily in his heart. He must have moved forward because both his father and the cat moved to stop him. An arm fell over his shoulder and a sharp claw scraped at his leg.

"Do not look James, hide your face away. Remember your mother in a better light. She is a proud, dutiful woman, who believes in God and his mercy. If she believes it is her time to join him, then she will have accepted her fate. And she will be joining him in heaven, James. Be sure of that." His father's voice cracked slightly at the end of his speech, but James knew that he meant and believed every word.

An official stepped forward and began to read the charges of which Mary Tyler had been found guilty. The hangman moved into place; arms raised ready to release the floor of the platform where Mrs Tyler stood. The crowd began to whisper prayers and incantations. James and his family looked on, barely dry-eyed but determined. Just do it, James thought. Release the floor; let my mother's soul fly to heaven, where it belongs. No-one should suffer this wait, least of all her. He closed his eyes as the tears squeezed under his lashes and through his head ran pictures of the part he had played in this disaster. Like an endless dream sequence, the events played over and over again. Please do it now, he begged.

Then quietly, but clearly a voice was heard above the rest, gently reciting, gently praying.

"Our father which art in heaven, hallowed be thy name. Thy kingdom come; thy will be done on earth…" The crowd gasped and then was stunned into silence and even the official stopped his reading. They listened attentively, as Mary Tyler perfectly recited the whole of the Lord's Prayer, hands clasped tightly in front of her. Those around them gasped again in disbelief. A man pushed forward,

"This is not right," he shouted. A witch cannot recite the Lord's Prayer."

"Impossible!" exclaimed another.
Mary Tyler stood still and repeated the prayer, hands still clasped, eyes closed, ready for the floor to fall away.

"She is NOT a witch," a woman breathed, as the evidence before their eyes took hold.

The crowd surged forward, better to see the woman who was not a witch. The hangman looked uncertain, should he press the button? James saw him hesitate; his hand close to the button. He was going to push it, anyway! James pulled away from his father, pushing his way through the crowd, intending to knock down the hangman if necessary. Stop him, to give everyone time to think. He had almost reached his target, when a man moved onto the platform, removing the noose from his mother's neck. He raised a quieting hand,

"Brothers and Sisters, we must stop the execution, until such times as this can be investigated," the magistrate said in an official tone. "No witch is able to recite the Lord's Prayer, so unless trickery is at work here, Mary Tyler may be innocent." He instructed the guards to return her to the prison until the courts had discussed this new evidence and made judgment on her fate.

As she was led away, the magistrate again addressed the gathering.

"This is not to say that all prisoners are innocent and further judgments and executions will not be affected by today's event."

Taking note of his warning, James knew that even if his mother was saved, then Rebecca could not rely on a similar conclusion. He looked down at the tortoiseshell cat and knew then that to be sure of saving her, he must persuade her to leave Salem for good.

Chapter Twenty-Five

Escape Again

Returning to their home, both Tyler children were thinking of the events they had witnessed. James' father took no notice of the stray cat that followed them. They talked little as they walked. James had to see to his chores before he could join Rebecca in the barn, by which time it was clear that she was agitated and ready to be returned to herself. James explained how and Rebecca soon changed back, stretching as she did so. Neither of them discussed their time at Gallows' Hill or its surprising outcome. Both knew that little more could be done. Their mother's fate lay in the hands of the magistrate and God.

Talking quietly, both minds turned to the subject of Rebecca's escape. The guards would surely have found her missing by now and even with the strange events on the hill, they would come looking for her.

"Rebecca," James spoke quietly. "You realize that you must not stay here, you must leave Salem for good."
Ready to deny this, she thought better and said,

"Will you come with me, James? I know your life here is not happy and father will be spending all his time trying to save mother. You have nothing to keep you here."

James knew the truth of these words. When everything settled down, as it surely must, whatever the fate of their mother, James was still too different to fit comfortably into the life of a small village. He nodded his head and it was settled.

Later that night the great banging at the door came again and the magistrate searched the house and the barn for his missing prisoner. All he found were a man and a boy in the house and a tortoiseshell cat sleeping in the barn. He went away disappointed. When darkness was at its most dense, James crept from his bed and with a small knife carved on the kitchen table, 'Rebecca is safe' and then he and his sister set off to put as many miles as they could between them and Salem, before the first light of dawn broke through. When his father awoke, startled by the silence of the house, he found the carving and smiled. While he gently planed the words away, he smiled again, knowing James and his daughter were together, safely away from the witch trials. He hoped with all his heart that they remained safe, but knew that if they were to ever return or he to find them then both their lives would be in danger.

James and his sister travelled light. He had bundled a few clothes, some chunks of bread and of course the box, spell book and pendant into a cloth which he carried on his shoulder. He had considered returning these magical items to the ground, but had decided that they might be useful on their journey. They walked and walked until their feet were sore, but by morning they had put enough distance between them and the dreadful place Salem had become. They journeyed for weeks, walking, working where they could, even begging when they had no food. Their goal was to reach the governor's house to plead the case of Salem and its innocent victims. Plans made on their journey kept them going to their ultimate destination.

Chapter Twenty-Six

The Governor's Part

The story of Salem and its witch trials had reached the governor's house before them. The whole of Massachusetts had been alerted to the terrible happenings in that fated village. Everyone was willing to stop and talk in shocked tones, to tell the two Tyler children of the stories that had come from their home. They learned that the accusations had not stopped when they had left. More people had been imprisoned, hanged or crushed to death. Each tale was told in total belief and with accusing eyes. However, there was no news of their mother and they took heart from this, believing if not freed then surely she was still alive.

James and Rebecca tried to reach the governor to plead with him to stop the accusations which were destroying their home. Every door was barred, every avenue closed to them. Both had tried to use the spell to gain entrance to the house, but it seemed it was not easy, even for a cat to enter such an important place. Then one day, when they were walking in the street outside the governor's house, a wave of incredible news flooded through their surroundings. Women on the street passed on the news and eventually it reached James and Rebecca's ears.

"The girls in Salem have accused the governor's wife of witchcraft," a woman cried disparagingly. A buzz of disbelief filled Massachusetts. Stories of innocence spread, and public opinion began to change. No-one believed the stories the girls told anymore. People began to doubt the evidence which was always vague and circumstantial. Important respected men, like Increase Mather, president of Harvard College, spoke out against the accusations and insisted it was better to release one witch than to accuse ten innocent victims.

Suddenly everyone wanted to hear the dreadful tales of Salem, especially from the mouth of an eyewitness. James and Rebecca were now invited to meet Governor Phipps, who listened carefully and patiently to their recounts of Salem, their mother and imprisonment. They convinced him that there was no real evidence and that it was all started by frightened girls accusing rather than being punished. He listened and then investigated further and to their relief prevented any more accusations and arrests being made, based on such flimsy evidence. The remaining accused witches of Salem were released, including Mary Tyler. Tituba, still imprisoned was sold to a new master and Reverend Parris was removed from the church and replaced. James and Rebecca were both thankful and relieved.

In the spring of 1697, a full five years after the original accusations, Rebecca, despite having become maid to the governor's wife, happily returned to Salem to join her parents, to live her days on the farm which she eventually inherited. And James, well, even though his parents begged him to return, having learned so effectively that his differences would never allow him to fit into a small village life, decided to remain in the governor's house, where he had also secured a job. Some say, he did rather well for himself, despite his peculiar looks.

The spell book and pendant? James secreted those away, ready to be used if necessary. Allegedly, he never needed the spell again, but a pure, white cat with pink eyes was often glimpsed along the corridors of the governor's house. Was it him? Is that how he did so well for himself? Who knows? Perhaps!

Printed in Great Britain
by Amazon

25975526R00057